Goat

in a

Boat

by Janee Trasler

ACORN™
SCHOLASTIC INC.

For Jason, my favorite bunny guy.

Library of Congress Cataloging-in-Publication Data

Names: Trasler, Janee, author, illustrator. Title: Goat in a boat / Janee Trasler. Description: First edition. | New York : Acorn/Scholastic Inc., 2020. | Series: A Frog and Dog book ; [2] | Audience: Ages 4–6. | Audience: Grades K–1. | Summary: When Goat appears wearing a raincoat and invites all the animals to go for a boat ride on a sunny day, Dog declines but as heavy rain falls, Dog needs a boat, too. Identifiers: LCCN 2019048955 | ISBN 9781338540420 (paperback) | ISBN 9781338540451 (library binding) Subjects: CYAC: Rain and rainfall–Fiction. | Boats and boating–Fiction. | Floods–Fiction. | Frogs–Fiction. | Dogs–Fiction. | Friendship–Fiction. Classification: LCC PZ7.T6872 Go 2020 | DDC [E]–dc23 LC record available at https://lccn.loc.gov/2019048955ISBN

10 9 8 7 6 5 4 3   20 21 22 23 24

Printed in China   62

First edition, May 2020

Edited by Rachel Matson

Book design by Sunny Lee

Goat

Frog

Frog

Frog

1

Here comes Goat.

5

6

7

Boat

Here comes Goat.

In a boat.

Who wants a ride?

18

There they go.

Rain

Here comes the rain.

23

Dog needs a boat.

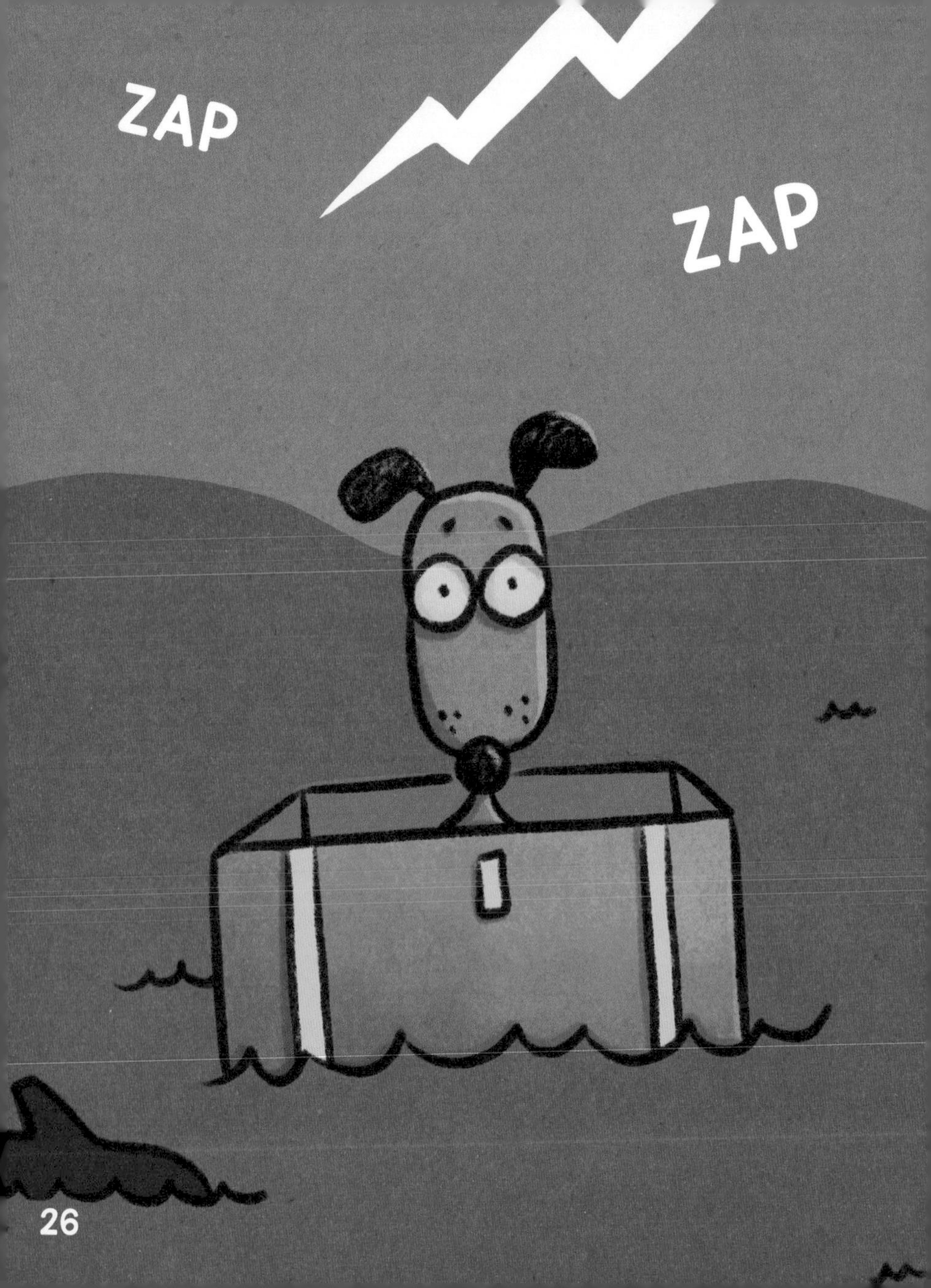
ZAP
ZAP

It is dark.
Is that a...

28

SHARK!

BARK BARK BARK!

29

It is not a shark.

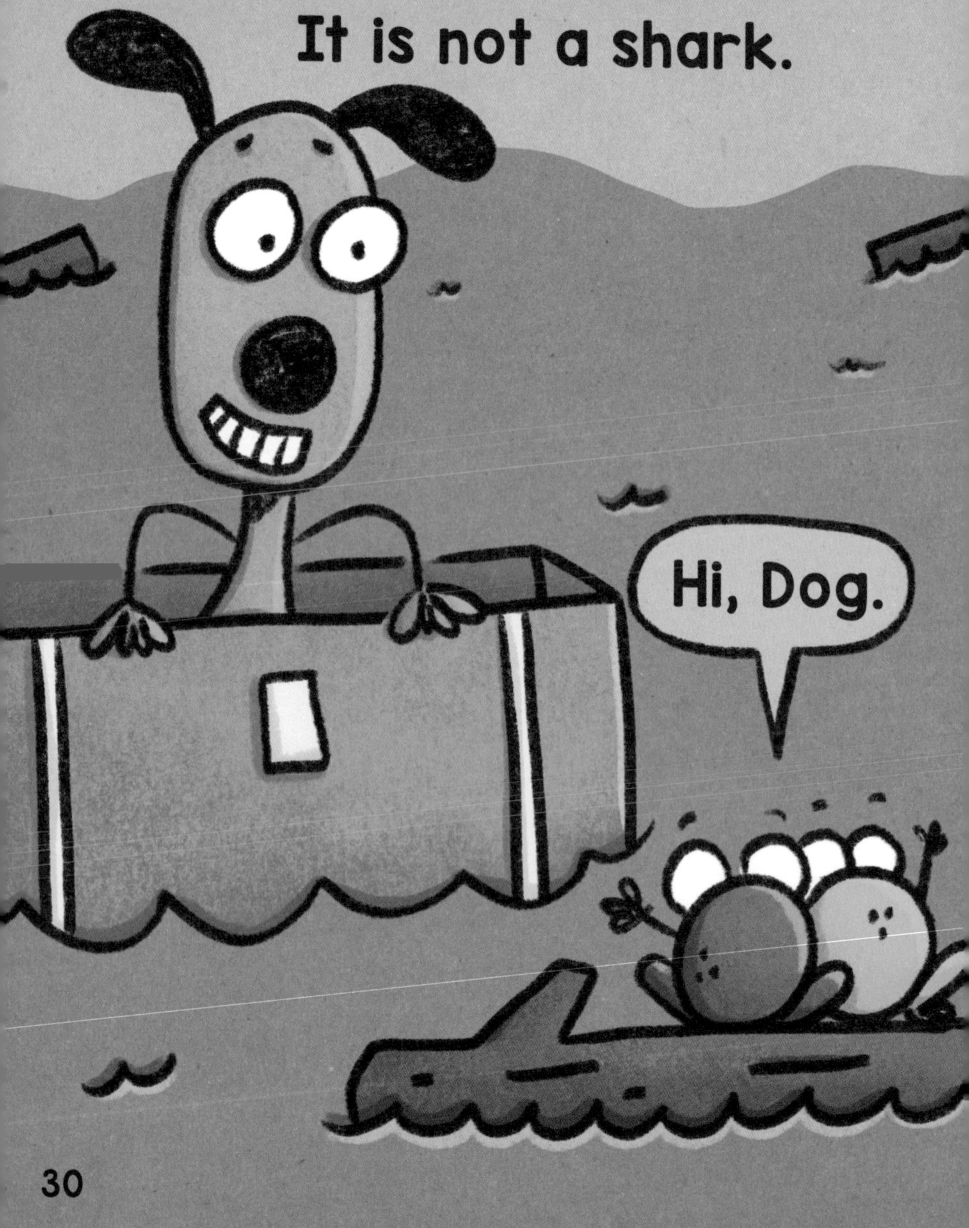

Safe

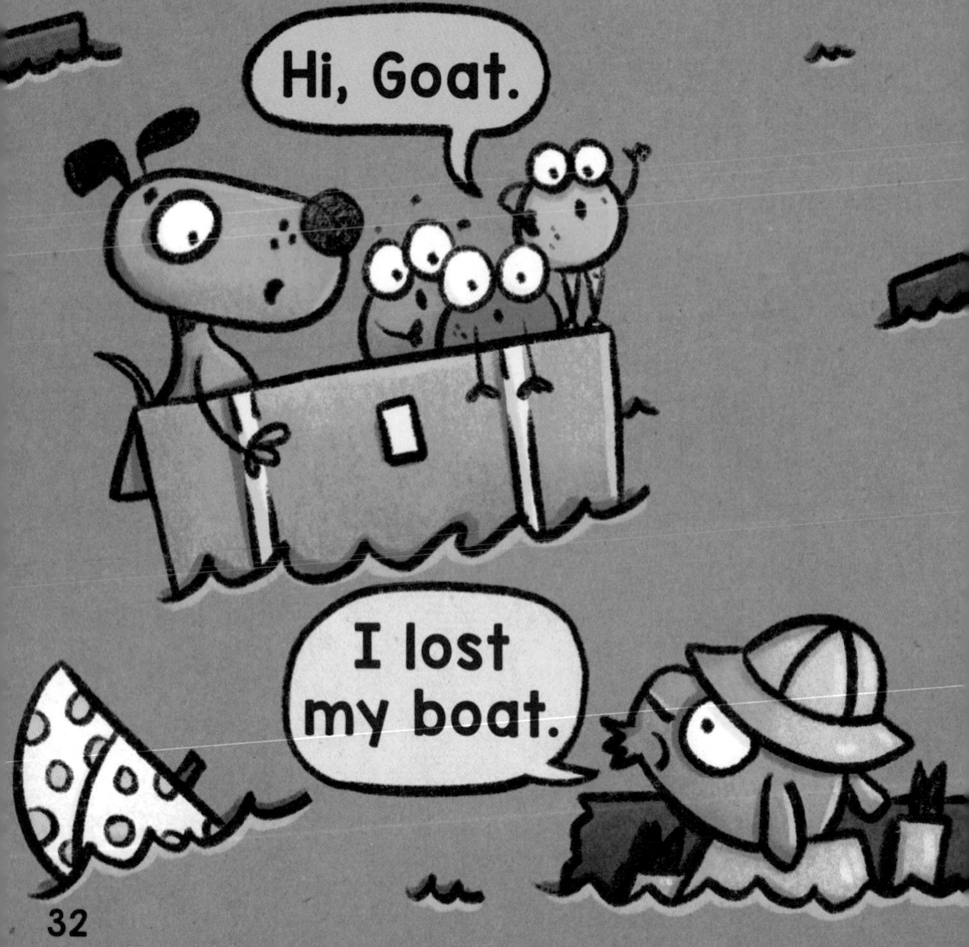

Go Dog, go!

35

Dog saves the day.

41

43

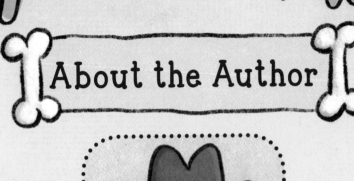

About the Author

Janee Trasler loves to make kids laugh. Whether she is writing books, drawing pictures, singing songs, or performing with her puppets, she is going for the giggle. Janee lives in Texas with her hubby, her doggies, and one very squeaky guinea pig.

YOU CAN DRAW DOG!

1 Draw a long oval.

2 Draw a sideways figure 8. Add a dot in the middle of each circle.

3 Draw two half-circles for the eyebrows.

4 Add a circle at the bottom for the nose.

5 Draw two ovals. Connect them to the head with a line.

6 Color in your drawing!

WHAT'S YOUR STORY?

Goat takes everyone on a boat ride.
Imagine **you** are going for a ride with Goat.
Where would you like to go?
Write and draw your story!